Kim's Trip

Clang, clang!
Ding, ding!
Chug, chug.
Bells ring.
Big Red sits on the tracks.

Kim and Mom step up
onto Big Red.
Mom gives their trunk
to Mr. Scott.
Big Red begins to move.

"Hang on!" yells Mr. Scott.
Kim and Mom sit down.
Big Red goes fast.
It chugs past ponds and dells.

It goes down hills.
The hills are big.
Kim and Mom look back.
The hills shrink as Big Red
goes past.

"Look!" says Mom.
"I think I see a skunk."
Kim looks.

"The skunk is gone, Mom,"
she says.
"I see a fox running
into a log."
Big Red begins to stop.
It has to link up
with Tuff Tim.

Mom and Kim get
off the train.
They get drinks and chips
at the shop.
They are quick.
It is not a long stop.

Clang, clang!
Ding, ding!
Chug, chug.
Bells ring.

Mom and Kim rush back
to Big Red.
They bring their drinks
with them.

They sit down.
Big Red sets off again.
Chug, chug!
"I just love trains,"
Kim tells Mom.

Drums and Pans

Jig was sad when he spoke.
"A brick fell on my drum.
It broke! It made a big hole
in the drum."
Jig, the pig, was very glum.

Nip said, "Let me think a bit.
We have to have
a thing to hit.
Can we take this box?
Can we bang on it with
a pipe or rocks?"

They did, but the box
was not like a drum.
It went crack, crack, crack,
and was not much fun.
Nip said, "The box is soft."

"It does not bang.
What do we have
that will ring and clang?"
Jig said, "By the stove there
is a thin, flat thing.
I use it to bake."

"Will it bang and ring?"
Jig held it up and hit it.
Clang!
But it was just a bit
of a bang.

15

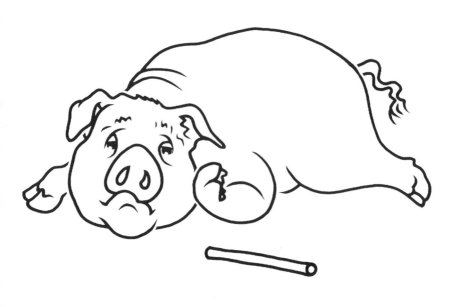

He hit it with a big, big
whack!
But that was just more
like a "Crack!"
Nip said, "What in this den
will bang and ring?"

"I cannot think
of even one thing."
Jig jumped up.
"I have a plan!"
He went and got a big
tin pan.

Jig said, "We can hit this pan.
It can bang and ring. It can!"
The pan did not bang
just like a drum.
But Nip and Jig
had lots of fun!

Mot Gets A Home

Mot, the bug, went home
with Kim.
Mot was in Kim's lunch bag!

Kim set the bag on the rug.
Mot crept up the side
of the bag.
At the top, Mot gave her
wings a stretch.
With a flap and a glide,
off she went!

Where did Mot land?
On the back of Gus, the cat!
Mot made Gus jump.
Gus did not like
a big bug on his back!
He did shake and twitch and
quake to get the bug off.

Then Gus ran to Kim.
Mot hung on to Gus
and went for a ride!
"Why is Gus so mad?"
said Kim.

"Why does he shake
and quake?
Does he have an itch?"
Kim gave Gus a pat
on the back.

She felt Mot with her hand.
"Yipe!" she said.
"It is the bug on the cat!"

Kim's mom came to her.
Mom said, "Let me check
that big bug."

She gave that bug
an up-close gaze.
"I think this will munch
on bad bugs.
I have a lime plant that
has bad bugs on it."

"Those bad bugs
make the lime plant sick.
Let me put Mot
on the lime plant.
She will like the bugs as
much as jam and punch."
So Mom put Mot
on the lime plant.

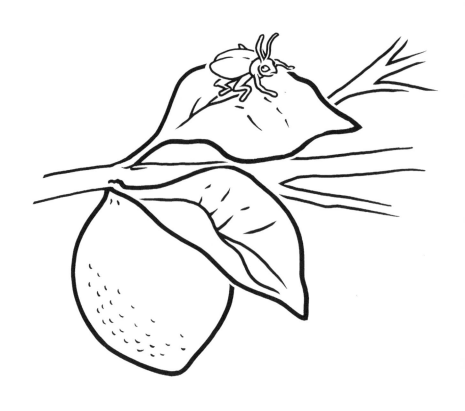

Mot was so glad.
This was the best
home for Mot.
She had a plant
with the bugs she
liked to munch best!

A Date with Dazz

Jig, the pig, and Nip, the fox,
have a date.
They do not wish to be late.
They must cross
a bunch of mud.
They slip and slide, with
a smack and a thud!

They are up to their necks
in slime.
Still they have a fine,
fine time.
Jig thinks the slime
is a game!
Nip thinks a mud slide
is the same!

They get to the home of
Dazz, the duck.
She will not let them in
with all that muck!
So they wipe off the mud
and grime.
They get rid of the muck
and the slime.

They go into Dazz's home
to dine.
They are pals,
and that is fine!

Stories by Susan Ebbers (Kim's Trip) and Sue Jones
(Drums and Pans, Mot Gets a Home, A Date with Dazz)
Illustrations by Deborah Wolfe Ltd.

Volume 19, ISBN: 1-931728-20-8

unleash the xPotential

ISBN 1-931728-20-8

phonics

PhonicsWorks™ Reader

26

Table of Contents